MORE GREAT GRAPHIC NOVEL SERIES AVAILABLE FROM
PAPERCUTᴢ™

THE SMURFS TALES

BRINA THE CAT

CAT & CAT

THE SISTERS

ATTACK OF THE STUFF

LOLA'S SUPER CLUB

SCHOOL FOR EXTRATERRESTRIAL GIRLS

GERONIMO STILTON REPORTER

THE MYTHICS

GUMBY

MELOWY

BLUEBEARD

GILLBERT

ASTERIX

FUZZY BASEBALL

THE CASAGRANDES

THE LOUD HOUSE

ASTRO MOUSE AND LIGHT BULB

GEEKY F@B 5

THE ONLY LIVING GIRL

papercutz.com
Also available where ebooks are sold.

BACK TO SCHOOL SPECIAL

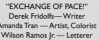

nickelodeon | THE LOUD HOUSE | "BACK TO SCHOOL SPECIAL"

KIERNAN SJURSEN-LIEN — Cover Artist

JAYJAY JACKSON — Design

KARA FEIN, CAITLIN FEIN, KRISTEN G. SMITH, DANA CLUVERIUS, MOLLIE FREILICH, NEIL WADE, MIGUEL PUGA,
LALO ALCARAZ, JOAN HILTY, KRISTEN YU-UM, EMILIE CRUZ, and ARTHUR "DJ" DESIN— Special Thanks

KARLO ANTUNES — Editor

STEPHANIE BROOKS — Assistant Managing Editor

JEFF WHITMAN — Comics Editor/Nickelodeon

MICOL HIATT — Comics Designer/Nickelodeon

JIM SALICRUP
Editor-in-Chief

ISBN: 978-1-5458-0891-7 paperback edition
ISBN: 978-1-5458-0890-0 hardcover edition

Papercutz books may be purchased for business or promotional use. For information on bulk purchases please contact Macmillan Corporate and Premium Sales Department at (800) 221-7945 x5442.

Printed in India
June 2022

Distributed by Macmillan
First Printing

MEET THE LOUD FAMILY
and friends!

LINCOLN LOUD
THE MIDDLE CHILD

Lincoln is the middle child, with five older sisters and five younger sisters. He has learned that surviving the Loud household means staying a step ahead. He's the man with a plan, always coming up with a way to get what he wants or deal with a problem, even if things inevitably go wrong. Being the only boy comes with some perks. Lincoln gets his own room — even if it's just a converted linen closet. On the other hand, being the only boy also means he sometimes gets a little too much attention from his sisters. They mother him, tease him, and use him as the occasional lab rat or fashion show participant. Lincoln's sisters may drive him crazy, but he loves them and is always willing to help out if they need him.

LORI LOUD
THE OLDEST

As the first-born child of the Loud Clan, Lori sees herself as the boss of all her siblings. She feels she's paved the way for them and deserves extra respect. Her signature traits are rolling her eyes, texting her boyfriend, Bobby, and literally saying "literally" all the time. Because she's the oldest and most experienced sibling, Lori can be a great ally, so it pays to stay on her good side, especially since she can drive.

LENI LOUD
THE FASHIONISTA

Leni spends most of her time designing outfits and accessorizing. She always falls for Luan's pranks, and sometimes walks into walls when she's talking (she's not great at doing two things at once). Leni might be flighty, but she's the sweetest of the Loud siblings and truly has a heart of gold (even though she's pretty sure it's a heart of blood).

LUNA LOUD
THE ROCK STAR

Luna is loud, boisterous, freewheeling, and her energy is always cranked to 11. She thinks about music so much that she even talks in song lyrics. On the off-chance she doesn't have her guitar with her, everything can and will be turned into a musical instrument. You can always count on Luna to help out, and she'll do most anything you ask, as long as you're okay with her supplying a rocking guitar accompaniment.

MR COCONUTS

Luan Loud's wise-cracking dummy.

LUAN LOUD
THE JOKESTER

Luan's a standup comedienne who provides a non-stop barrage of silly puns. She's big on prop comedy too – squirting flowers and whoopee cushions – so you have to be on your toes whenever she's around. She loves to pull pranks and is a really good ventriloquist – she is often found doing bits with her dummy, Mr. Coconuts. Luan never lets anything get her down; to her, laughter IS the best medicine.

LYNN LOUD
THE ATHLETE

Lynn is athletic and full of energy and is always looking for a teammate. With her, it's all sports all the time. She'll turn anything into a sport. Putting away eggs? Jump shot! Score! Cleaning up the eggs? Slap shot! Score! Lynn is very competitive, but despite her competitive nature, she always tries to just have a good time.

LOLA LOUD
THE BEAUTY QUEEN)

Lola could not be more different from her twin sister, Lana. She's a pageant powerhouse whose interests include glitter, photo shoots, and her own beautiful, beautiful face. But don't let her cute, gap-toothed smile fool you; underneath all the sugar and spice lurks a Machiavellian mastermind. Whatever Lola wants, Lola gets – or else. She's the eyes and ears of the household and never resists an opportunity to tattle on troublemakers. But if you stay on Lola's good side, you've got yourself a fierce ally – and a lifetime supply of free makeovers.

LUCY LOUD
THE EMO

You can always count on Lucy to give the morbid point of view in any given situation. She is obsessed with all things spooky and dark – funerals, vampires, séances, and the like. She wears mostly black and writes moody poetry. She's usually quiet and keeps to herself. Lucy has a way of mysteriously appearing out of nowhere, and try as they might, her siblings never get used to this.

LANA LOUD
THE TOMBOY

Lana is the rough-and-tumble sparkplug counterpart to her twin sister, Lola. She's all about reptiles, mud pies, and muffler repair. She's the resident Ms. Fix-it and is always ready to lend a hand – the dirtier the job, the better. Need your toilet unclogged? Snake fed? Back-zit popped? Lana's your gal. All she asks in return is a little A-B-C gum, or a handful of kibble (she often sneaks it from the dog bowl).

LISA LOUD
THE GENIUS

Lisa is smarter than the rest of her siblings combined. She'll most likely be a rocket scientist, or a brain surgeon, or an evil genius who takes over the world. Lisa spends most of her time working in her lab (the family has gotten used to the explosions), and says her research leaves little time for frivolous human pursuits like "playing" or "getting haircuts." That said, she's always there to help with a homework question, or to explain why the sky is blue, or to point out the structural flaws in someone's pillow fort. Lisa says it's the least she can do for her favorite test subjects, er, siblings.

LILY LOUD
THE BABY

Lily's the baby of the family, but she's growing up fast. She's a toddler now and can speak full sentences – well, sometimes. As an infant she was already mischievous, but now she's upped her game. No matter what, though, she still brings a smile to everyone's faces, and the family loves her unconditionally.

CHARLES

WALT

CLIFF

GEO

RITA LOUD

Mother to the eleven Loud kids, Mom (Rita Loud) wears many different hats. She's a chauffeur, homework-checker, and barf-cleaner-upper all rolled into one. She's always there for her kids and ready to jump into action during a crisis, whether it's a fight between the twins or Leni's missing shoe. When she's not chasing the kids around or at her day job as a dental hygienist, Mom pursues her passion: writing. She also loves taking on house projects and is very handy with tools (guess that's where Lana gets it from). Between writing, working, and being a mom, her days are always hectic but she wouldn't have it any other way.

LYNN LOUD SR.

Dad (Lynn Loud Sr.) is a fun-loving, upbeat aspiring chef. A kid-at-heart, he's not above taking part in the kids' zany schemes. In addition to cooking, Dad loves his van, playing the cowbell, and making puns. Before meeting Mom, Dad spent a semester in England and has been obsessed with British culture ever since – and sometimes "accidentally" slips into a British accent. When Dad's not wrangling the kids, he's pursuing his dream of opening his own restaurant where he hopes to make his "Lynn-sagnas" world-famous.

CLYDE McBRIDE
THE BEST FRIEND

Clyde is Lincoln's partner in crime. He's always willing to go along with Lincoln's crazy schemes (even if he sees the flaws in them up-front). Lincoln and Clyde are two peas in a pod and share pretty much all of the same tastes in movies, comics, TV shows, toys – you name it. As an only child, Clyde envies Lincoln – how cool would it be to always have siblings around to talk to? But since Clyde spends so much time at the Loud household, he's almost an honorary sibling anyway.

ZACH GURDLE

Zach is a self-admitted nerd who's obsessed with aliens and conspiracy theories. He lives between a freeway and a circus, so the chaos of the Loud House doesn't faze him. He and Rusty occasionally butt heads, but deep down, it's all love.

RUSTY SPOKES

Rusty is a self-proclaimed ladies' man who's always the first to dish out girl advice – even though he's never been on an actual date. His dad owns a suit rental service, so occasionally Rusty can hook the gang up with some dapper duds – just as long as no one gets anything dirty.

LIAM HUNNICUTT

Liam is an enthusiastic, sweet-natured farm boy full of down-home wisdom. He loves hanging out with his Mee Maw, wrestling his prize pig Virginia, and sharing his farm-to-table produce with the rest of the gang.

STELLA ZHAU

Stella, is a quirky, carefree girl who's new to Royal Woods. She has tons of interests, such as trying on wigs, playing laser tag, eating curly fries, and hanging with her friends. But what she loves the most is tech — she always wants to dismantle electronics and put them back together again.

RONNIE ANNE SANTIAGO

Ronnie Anne's a skateboarding city girl now. She's fearless, free-spirited, and always quick to come up with a plan. She's one tough cookie, but she also has a sweet side. Ronnie Anne loves helping her family, and that's taught her to help others, too. When she's not pitching in at the family *mercado*, you can find her exploring the neighborhood with her best friend Sid, or ordering hot dogs with her skater buds Casey, Nikki, and Sameer.

BOBBY SANTIAGO

Bobby is Ronnie Anne's big bro. He's a student and one of the hardest workers in the city! He loves his family and loves working at the *mercado*. As his *abuelo's* right hand man, Bobby can't wait to take over the family business one day. He's a big kid at heart, and his clumsiness gets him into some sticky situations at work, like locking himself in the freezer. *Mercado* mishaps aside, everyone in the neighborhood loves to come to the store and talk to Bobby.

MARIA CASAGRANDE SANTIAGO

She's the mother of Bobby and Ronnie Anne. A hardworking nurse, she doesn't get to spend a lot of time with her kids, but when she does she treasures it. Maria is calm and rational but often worries about whether she's doing enough for her kids. Maria, Bobby, and Ronnie Anne are a close-knit trio who were used to having only each other – until they moved in with their extended family.

HECTOR CASAGRANDE

Hector is Carlos and Maria's dad, and the *abuelo* of the family (that means grandpa)! He owns the *mercado* on the ground floor of their apartment building and takes great pride in his work, his family, and being the unofficial "mayor" of the block. He loves to tell stories, share his ideas, and gossip (even though he won't admit to it). You can find him working in the *mercado*, playing guitar, or watching his favorite *telenovela*.

ROSA CASAGRANDE

Rosa is Carlos and Maria's mom and the *abuela* of the family (that means grandma)! She's the head of the household, the wisest Casagrande, and the master cook with a superhuman ability to tell when anyone in the house is hungry. She often tries to fix problems or illnesses with traditional Mexican home remedies and potions. She's very protective of her family... sometimes a little too much.

SERGIO

Sergio is the Casagrandes' beloved pet parrot. He's a blunt, sassy bird who "thinks" he's full of wisdom and always has something to say. The Casagrandes have to keep a close eye on their credit card as Sergio is addicted to online shopping and is always asking the family to buy him some new gadget he saw on TV. Sergio is most loyal to Rosa and serves as her wing-man, partner in crime, taste tester, and confidant. He can be found trying to get his ex-girlfriend, Priscilla (an ostrich at the zoo), to respond to him.

CARLOS CASAGRANDE

Carlos is Maria's brother. He's married to Frida, and together they have four kids: Carlota, C.J., Carl, and Carlitos. Carlos is a Professor of Cultural Studies at a local college. Usually he has his head in the clouds or his nose in a textbook. Relatively easygoing, Carlos is a loving father and an enthusiastic teacher who tries to get his kids interested in their Mexican heritage.

FRIDA PUGA CASAGRANDE

Frida is Carlos, C.J., Carl, and Carlitos' mom. She's an art professor and a performance artist, and is always looking for new ways to express herself. She's got a big heart and isn't shy about her emotions. Frida tends to cry when she's sad, happy, angry, or any other emotion you can think of. She's always up for fun, is passionate about her art, and loves her family more than anything.

CARLOTA CASAGRANDE

Carlota is CJ, Carl, and Carlitos' older sister. A social media influencer, she's excited to be like a big sister to Ronnie Anne. She's a force to be reckoned with, and is always trying to share her distinctive vintage style tips with Ronnie Anne.

CARLITOS CASAGRANDE

Carlitos is the baby of the family, and is always copying the behavior of everyone in the household – even if they aren't human. He's a playful and silly baby who loves to play with the family pets.

CJ (CARLOS JR.) CASAGRANDE

CJ is Carlota's younger brother and Carl and Carlitos' older brother. He was born with Down Syndrome. He lights up any room with his infectious smile and is always ready to play. He's obsessed with pirates and is BFFs with Bobby. He likes to wear a bowtie to any family occasion, and you can always catch him laughing or helping his *abuela*.

CARL CASAGRANDE

Carl is wise beyond his years. He's confident, outgoing, and puts a lot of time and effort into looking good. He likes to think of himself as a suave businessman and doesn't like to get caught playing with his action figures or wearing his footie PJs. Even though Bobby is nothing but nice to him, Carl sees his big cousin as his biggest rival.

LALO

Lalo is a slobbery bull mastiff who thinks he's a lapdog. He's not the smartest pup and gets scared easily… but he loves his family and loves to cuddle.

HAIKU | MORPHEUS | PERSEPHONE | DANTE | BERTRAND | BORIS

MORTICIANS CLUB

MS. GALIANO

Ms. Galiano is Ronnie Anne and the skater kids' teacher at Cesar Chavez Academy. She is sweet as pie and often relies on the kids to keep her up to date on the new, hip, pop culture trends. She briefly dated Ronnie Anne's dad, Arturo, and even though it didn't work out, they still remain friends.

COACH CRAWFORD

Coach Crawford is Cesar Chavez Academy's gruff PE teacher. Militant in his approach and a traditionalist as far as what he considers a "sport," Coach Crawford is willing to adjust his stance on things if it means he can just drink his coffee in peace. Now in retirement, Coach Crawford stays active by occasionally subbing in for new PE teacher, Mrs. Kernicky, much to the dismay of the students.

CHERYL FARRELL

Cheryl is the secretary at Royal Woods Elementary School and identical twin to Meryl, who lovingly calls her "Cher-Bear!" She is a bubbly Southerner who is always rooting for the students at Royal Woods Elementary. She loves boot scootin', storing items in her signature beehive hairdo, and watching soap operas with her sister in their shared condo.

MERYL FARRELL

Meryl is the secretary at Royal Woods Middle School and identical twin to Cheryl. Like her sister, she is a charming Southerner and loves gossip, karaoke, and soap operas. She has a sweet way of talking (comparing things to baked goods) and is always eager to help students when they need her.

PRINCIPAL RAMIREZ

Principal Ramirez runs Royal Woods Middle School. She is firm when she needs to be but also super enthusiastic with the students, always there to cheer them on. She's got a soft spot for the school's Action News Team, no matter how many times their shenanigans make her life difficult. And she's always open to creative problem solving, even if it means temporarily sending Lincoln to a school in Canada!

MRS. SALTER

Mrs. Salter is the most popular teacher at Royal Woods Middle School due to her classroom juice bar. Mrs. Salter is a free spirit who has a passion for making education fun! Rusty, Liam, Clyde, Zach, and Stella are lucky enough to be her students while Lincoln has to watch the fun from afar in Mr. Bolhofner's class...

MR. BOLHOFNER

Mr. Bolhofner is Lincoln's gruff but well-meaning middle school teacher, whose stories of survival out in the wild are renowned throughout Royal Woods. He has a passion for smoked jerky and taxidermy, and a flair for playing the bass drum. He has two fierce pets that usually cause trouble at school: a piranha named Hank and a bobcat named Rocket. Although school rumors suggest that Bolhofner is scary enough to warrant the nickname "Skullhofner," Lincoln and his friends know that there's a big softie underneath his hard exterior.

DR. SHUTTLEWORTH

Dr. Shuttleworth runs the prestigious Baby Bunker Preschool, where Lily is a student. She is a kind, sophisticated educator who expresses pride in her students and encourages creativity and good manners. If you want to be in her class, you better be potty-trained!

"DODGE HALL!"

ARE WE REALLY GOING TO DO THIS?

IT'S THE ULTIMATE DARE, *CLYDE*. RUN ACROSS TO THE OTHER SIDE AND AVOID THE HALL MONITOR. WHO'S FIRST?

THIS AIN'T MY FIRST RODEO.

NICE ROPING, *LYNN!*

YEE-HAW.

ALIENS EXIST! I KNEW IT!

THE ONLY UFO HERE IS YOUR UNFORTUNATE FAILED OPERATION.

TIME TO WIN THIS DARE.

CLICK

CLICK

OUR BEST CHANCE IS IF WE RUSH ACROSS TOGETHER. SHE CAN'T GET ALL OF US.

GO!

WE DID IT! WE--

THOP THOP THOP

NICE TRY, STINKIN'. BUT I KEEP THIS EMERGENCY LOCKER READY FOR JUST SUCH AN OCCASION.

ALL IN A DAY'S WORK FOR A HALL MONITOR.

END OF THE LINE

14

"BAD HAIR DAY!"

LENI! I NEED YOUR HELP. IT'S A HAIR-MERGENCY!

DID YOU TRY USING MY ROSE WATER MIST?

I'VE TRIED EVERYTHING.

I'M SORRY, LOLA. THERE'S ONLY ONE OPTION LEFT.

YOU DON'T MEAN...

SNIP

SNIP

"WAITING..."

WAIT A SEC, WHAT'S THIS LINE FOR?

75th Plaid Cup LEADERBOARD

OMG, THE *PLAID CUP* IS TODAY?

FINALLY, SOMETHING WORTH WAITING FOR!

SHHHHH!

SORRY!

END

"HOW YOU LIKE THEM APPLES?"

IT SEEMS WRONG TO GIVE THIS TO MY TEACHER. OR EAT IT MYSELF.

SO IT'S ALL YOURS, **MR. COCONUTS.** IN CASE YOU GET HUNGRY WHILE I'M AWAY.

SEE YOU AFTER SCHOOL!

BANANAS. TOO CHEERFUL.

DO YOU THINK HE LIKES ORANGES?

TAKE MY TAPIOCA PUDDING. YUCK!

WHAT HAVE WE HERE?

JACKPOT!

SO HOW WAS SCHOOL...?

WHOA, IT'S GONE! DID YOUR DOLL EAT ALL OUR FOOD?

NAH. MR. COCONUTS JUST FEEDS ON ATTENTION!

CLEARLY THERE'S GOT TO BE A SCIENTIFIC EXPLANATION FOR THIS.

EURP!

END

"IT SUITS YOU"

CHERYL, I CAN'T WAIT TO FIND THE PERFECT OUTFIT FOR THE KARAOKE IN THE PARK COMPETITION LATER TODAY.

I THINK WITH A NEW CARDIGAN AND A SET OF PEARLS, MERYL, WE'LL BE SWEETER THAN HONEY-PIE!

OR MAYBE...

...WE CAN TRY SOMETHING A LITTLE MORE OUTSIDE THE BOX?

ISN'T THIS THE MOST BEAUTIFUL THING YOU'VE EVER SEEN?

HMM...

OH, HONEY... NO...

PLEASE, TRY IT ON... FOR ME?

FINE! I'LL PROVE IT WON'T WORK. AND THEN WE'LL GO BACK TO PEEKING AT THE PEARLS.

END

"PARADE OF FOOLS"

ANY IDEAS FOR OUR SCHOOL PROJECT?

I DUNNO, FRANCE SEEMS BORING...

BORING?

FRANCE IS FULL OF SPOOKY STUFF! LOOK... THEY HAVE A WHOLE UNDERGROUND FILLED WITH *BONES!*

THEY'LL LET US DO THAT, *HAIKU?*

OUR TEACHER FAINTED DURING THE LAST SKELETON INCIDENT.

DANTE HAS A POINT...

WAIT, GUYS! I HAVE AN IDEA!

WHAT IF WE WROTE OUR PAPER ON MIMES? THEY DRESS JUST LIKE US!

OH, YEAH! THEY'RE KINDA GOTHIC!

The FRENCH FOOL

THEY'RE THE ONLY TYPE OF *CLOWN* I LIKE!

CLOWN CLOWN CLOWN... CLOWN CLOWN

BORIS HATES CLOWNS!

IT'S OKAY, BORIS, NOT EVERY CLOWN IS LIKE THE ONES YOU'RE SCARED OF.

YEAH, THEY CAN BE SCARY IN A FUN WAY, NOT JUST A *SCARY* WAY!

HERE, LOOK, I PROMISE THESE BOOKS CAN'T HURT YOU. YOU SEE THIS ONE?

BORIS SEES. BORIS DOES NOT LIKE.

SEE HERE? IT HELPS TO KNOW WHERE CLOWNS CAME FROM. THIS IS ONE OF THE FIRST. HE WAS CALLED *PIERROT!*

PIERROT

YEAH, AND THERE'RE MIMES, LIKE WE'VE BEEN STUDYING...

MIMES IN MOTION

ACTUALLY, MY UNCLE USED TO BE AN *"AUGUSTE CLOWN."* THAT'S THE KIND OF CLOWN WHO THE JOKE'S ALWAYS ON!

I MISS GETTING THE LEFTOVER PIES...

OH, THAT REMINDS ME!

WHEN I WAS LITTLE, WE USED TO GO TO RODEOS, AND THEY HAD THEIR OWN TYPE OF CLOWNS THERE!

THEY WOULD DO BRAVE THINGS NO ONE ELSE WOULD, JUST TO KEEP THE RODEO RIDERS SAFE!

I THINK MY FAVORITE IS THE CLASSIC JESTER...

THEY HAD TO PLEASE THEIR KING... FOR THEM, CLOWNERY WAS *LIFE OR DEATH!*

THEY WERE TRUE GOTHS AT HEART.

AND THERE'S EVEN THE WANDERING CLOWN...

A LONER WHO FINDS STORIES IN FAR-REACHING PLACES...

IF I WERE A CLOWN, MAYBE I WOULD WANT TO WANDER THE WORLD LIKE THAT. WHAT ABOUT YOU, BORIS?

THESE DON'T SOUND LIKE THE CLOWNS THAT SCARE BORIS...

PERHAPS BORIS NEED *NOT* BE AFRAID OF CLOWNS, AFTER ALL!

THAT'S THE SPIRIT! GO BORIS! YAAAAY.

SEE, EVEN THEIR WHITE FACEPAINT MATCHES YOU!

YES... BORIS FEELS... HAPPY!

HEY, EVERYONE...

HOW CAN YOU TELL A CLOWN JUST FARTED? THEY *SMELL FUNNY!*

EEEAAAAAAAGHHHHH!

SIGH. WELL, THAT WAS ALL FOR NAUGHT.

HE REALLY HATES *CLOWNING* AROUND, HUH? HA!

END

"PASS CLASS OR DASH"

OKAY, SID! YOU'LL KEEP A LOOK OUT, AND I'LL HANDLE THE REST. LET'S RIDE!

INCOMING!

FLIT

FLIT

FLIT

SPRANG

YOU DID IT, *RONNIE ANNE!* WAY TO GO!

ON OUR RIGHT! THREE DODGEBALLS COMING OUR WAY!

BOOM

BOOM

BOOM

PIECE OF CAKE!

⸗GULP!⸗ I DON'T THINK WE CAN HULA OUR WAY OUT OF THIS ONE!

ONE...

AT...

WE DID IT!

...A TIME!

GOOEY MOAT AHEAD! NOT GOOD, NOT GOOD!

COACH

SID! I CAN'T SEE!

RONNIE ANNE, DO SOMETHING!

I CAN'T! YOU HAVE TO GRAB THE ROPE!

YOU'RE MY BEST FRIEND. YOU CAN DO THIS!

OOH-RAAAAH!

I DID IT! I CAN'T BELIEVE IT! I DID IT!

CHAAANG... CASAAAAGRANDE!

AW, MAN...

NOT GOOD!

I'M SORRY, COACH. RONNIE ANNE WAS JUST TRYING TO HELP. I'M NOT THE MOST ATHLETIC PERSON--

THAT MIGHT BE TRUE, BUT GYM IS MORE THAN JUST BEING TOUGH OR ATHLETIC, IT'S ABOUT TRYING YOUR BEST.

⇒SNIFF!⇐ DOES THIS MEAN I FAIL?

NOT THIS TIME AROUND.

WHAT?

EVEN THOUGH YOU DIDN'T COMPLETE THE RELAY AS I WOULD HAVE HOPED... YOU STILL DID WORK AS A TEAM... AND YOU SUPPORTED EACH OTHER. THAT'S WHAT GYM IS ALL ABOUT. BESIDES NO TEAM HAS *EVER* PASSED.

PASSED

37

BUT... AS PUNISHMENT FOR NOT FOLLOWING MY EXACT INSTRUCTIONS, YOU'RE GOING TO HELP ME WITH A LITTLE SOMETHING.

?

ICE CREAM SUNDAES

THIS IS MUCH MORE MY SPEED, BUT NEXT YEAR I'M GOING TO TRY EVEN HARDER TO PASS GYM ON MY OWN.

THAT'S THE SPIRIT! AND YOU'RE STILL ON THE SKATE TEAM!

I'LL CHEERS TO THAT!

OKAY, THAT WAS A GOOD WARM UP...

NOW, HOW ABOUT YOU SCRAPE OUT THE *CHEWING GUM* MOAT. CAREFUL FOR *LAIRD'S* RETAINER...

END

"EXCHANGE OF PACE!"

AM I IN TROUBLE, *MRS. RAMIREZ?*

NOT AT ALL, *LINCOLN.* IN FACT, YOU'VE BEEN RANDOMLY SELECTED TO BE OUR SPECIAL EXCHANGE STUDENT.

I GUARANTEE YOU'LL HAVE AN AMAZING TIME!

AN EXCHANGE STUDENT? DIDN'T YOU GET KICKED OUT OF CANADA?

I'M GOING SOMEWHERE DIFFERENT. I JUST DON'T KNOW WHERE.

MAYBE TO JAPAN! I WONDER WHAT GYM CLASS IS LIKE THERE?

NAW, HE'S DEFINITELY GOING TO FASHION SCHOOL, LIKE IN MILAN.

SOME OF THE BEST SUITS MY FATHER RENTS CLAIM TO BE KNOCKOFFS FROM THERE.

I'D GIVE ANYTHING TO GO TO A NEW TECH SCHOOL, WITH ALL THE LATEST ELECTRONICS AND TECHNOLOGY.

YOUR TEACHER COULD EVEN BE AN ADVANCED ARTIFICIAL INTELLIGENCE!

NOT IF HE'S LEFT THE PLANET.

EVERYONE'S RIDING ROCKETS LATELY. I BET HE'S GOING TO SPACE SCHOOL ON THE MOON.

WHEREVER IT IS, I'M SURE IT'LL BE INTERESTING!

IS THIS A MISTAKE?

NO, SILLY. WELCOME TO YOUR NEW SCHOOL, LINCOLN!

THE BABY BUNKER PRESCHOOL?!

IT'S REALLY NO DIFFERENT THAN WATCHING *LILY* AT HOME. EXCEPT WITH MORE BABIES AROUND.

YOU'RE GOING TO HAVE SO MUCH FUN! IT'S ONLY FOR A WEEK. BUT YOU'LL BE HELPING OUT AS A FAVOR FOR A TEACHER I KNOW.

I GUESS IT CAN'T BE THAT BAD.

I WAS *SO* WRONG!

END

40

"TRAILER PORK"

GLAD TO HAVE YOU JOIN ME TODAY, *LINCOLN.*

YOU MADE ME, *MR. BOLHOFNER.* I'M ON LUNCH DETENTION.

A BAG LUNCH? THAT'S NO WAY TO EAT! KIDS THESE DAYS.

SO, UM...WHAT ARE *YOU* EATING TODAY, MR. BOLHOFNER?

I'M GLAD YOU ASKED. WE'RE GOING TO FIND OUT TOGETHER.

"WE"?!

HOW DO YOU THINK I SURVIVED IN THE JUNGLE USING ONLY A SPORK AND MY WITS?

IN MY DAY, WE HAD TO HUNT FOR OUR FOOD!

ANYTHING WORTH EATING IS WORTH CATCHING.

COME ON. KEEP UP!

BEFORE YOU CATCH IT, YOU MUST FIRST TRACK IT. USE YOUR SURROUNDINGS.

WILD BOARS LEAVE BEHIND HOOF PRINTS AND TUSK MARKS. IT'S LIKE WE'RE IN ANOTHER WORLD!

DID YOU SAY BOARS?!

TIME TO GET DIRTY.

BIKE TIRE MARKS?

DON'T WASTE OUR TIME WITH THOSE. BOARS ON BIKES ARE PREPOSTEROUS. TRUST ME.

MR. BOLHOFNER, I DON'T THINK THERE ARE ANY WILD BOARS HERE AT SCHOOL.

THAT'S RIGHT. YOU *DON'T* THINK. SO, *LOOK!*

PIGS LOVE TRASH. GET IN THERE AND SEARCH FOR CLUES.

UGH! NO WAY!

YOU'RE RIGHT. NO BOAR HERE. TODAY'S MENU IS MYSTERY MEAT.

LET'S GET TO THE BOTTOM OF THIS MYSTERY.

CAFETERIA

END

"STUDENT STORE LORE"

"A FRUITLESS ENDEAVOR"

MRS. SALTER'S JUICE BAR IS THE BEST!

YA CAN'T FAULT HER.

HEY, GUYS! CAN I GET ONE TOO?

SORRY, *LINC.* YOU KNOW THE RULES. YOU'RE ONLY ALLOWED IF YOU'RE ENROLLED IN MRS. SALTER'S CLASS.

ALL OTHER ATTEMPTS HAVE FAILED.

WE'LL SEE ABOUT THAT...

BZZZT
ACCESS DENIED

DANG IT!

CAN YOU CHECK AGAIN? I'M A TRANSFER STUDENT.

SORRY. YOU'RE NOT ON THE LIST.

JUST ONE DRINK, PLEEEEASE?

IMPOSSIBLE.

IMPORTANT SCHOOL ASSEMBLY...

ALL CLASSES ARE TO REPORT IMMEDIATELY TO THE GYMNASIUM!

NOW'S MY CHANCE!

YAY! ASSEMBLY!

HUP!

IT'S EVERYTHING THEY SAID IT WOULD BE. IT'S... ⇒SNIFF!⇐ GLORIOUS!

YOU'RE NOT ALLOWED TO HAVE THIS. THAT'S A DEMERIT, *STINKIN'*!

BUT YOU'RE NOT IN THIS CLASS EITHER, *LYNN*!

JUST ONE OF THE PERKS OF BEING HALL MONITOR.

EARTH

END

"SLEEPLESS IN PRESCHOOL"

TA-DA!

WOW! *LILY* SMART!

PLOP

GREAT JOB, MISS LILY. NOW LET'S PUT THE BLOCKS AWAY AND TRY OUT OUR NEW NAP MATS!

NIGHT, NIGHT!

CLICK

NAP TIME IS THE *PERFECT* TIME TO SORT CRAYONS!

SNORE!

=UGH!= TOO HARD!

SNORE!

50

"ALICE FORGIVEN"

SOMETHING LOOKS DIFFERENT, *CLYDE*. WHAT'S WITH ALL THESE POSTERS?

I'VE NEVER SEEN THEM BEFORE, *LINCOLN*. WHAT DO THEY SAY?

DEFINITELY SOMETHING STRANGE. HMMM...

HEY, DO YOU REMEMBER WHEN *M.A.L.I.C.E.* SENT THAT UNDERCOVER AGENT TO INFILTRATE *DAVID STEELE'S* SPY AGENCY?

YOU MEAN *VYPER SNAKEGRASS* IN THE DOUBLE DANGER AGENT INCIDENT!

≶GULP!≶ WHAT IF SOMEONE IS WORKING UNDERCOVER AT OUR SCHOOL?

M.A.L.I.C.E. DOES HAVE A PENCHANT FOR TRIANGLE SYMBOLISM. THEIR UNIFORMS, THEIR HIDDEN BASE IN BERMUDA. EVEN OUR GEOMETRY HOMEWORK.

M.A.L.I.C.E. STANDS FOR *MASTERMINDS ACTING LAWLESSLY IN COMMITTING EVIL.*

BUT WHAT ABOUT *"BALANCE?"*

BIG ARCHENEMY LURKING ALWAYS NEAR THE CAFETERIA EMINENTLY!

IT'S HER! *IT'S ALICE!*

I SEE YOU'VE ALREADY MET OUR NEW SUPERINTENDENT OF NUTRITION.

NUTRITION?!

THE BALANCE PROGRAM HELPS ENCOURAGE EATING A WELL BALANCED DIET AMONGST THE MAJOR FOOD GROUPS. ALL SYMBOLIZED IN THIS FOOD PYRAMID.

BALANCE

ANOTHER CRISIS AVERTED. GOOD JOB, AGENT McBRIDE.

WELL DONE, AGENT LOUD. ON TO OUR NEXT MISSION?

BALANCE

OF COURSE, TO UNLOCK THE SECRET OF NEXT WEEK'S CAFETERIA MENU!

M.A.L.I.C.E. End Transmission

"INTERSTELLA"

COME ON, WORK! I SPENT MY ENTIRE ALLOWANCE ON THIS.

HOW DO THEY EXPECT ME TO COMMUNICATE WITH THIS FAULTY UNIT?

MY PARENTS WARNED ME THIS WAS A WASTE OF MONEY.

AND MY FRIENDS WILL JUST MAKE FUN OF ME TOO.

IT'S ONLY JUNK!

CLUNK

HEY, *STELLA*, WHAT'S THAT?

A RADIO. *ZACH* JUST THREW IT AWAY.

I BELIEVE ZACH WAS TRYING TO USE IT TO TALK TO ALIENS. BUT I DON'T THINK IT WORKS THAT WAY.

BUT WHAT IF IT *COULD?*

YOU'VE GIVEN ME AN IDEA. I JUST NEED YOUR HELP TO DO IT.

"THE TEACHERS LOUNGE"

I'M SO THRILLED TO ANNOUNCE THAT DUE TO A SURPLUS IN THE BUDGET, WE HAVE A NEW...

LOUNGE CHAIR FOR THE TEACHERS LOUNGE!

OH, MY!

≷GASP!≶

FINALLY, SOMETHING COMFORTABLE TO EAT MY TUNA CASSEROLE ON!

NOW, TO SURPRISE CHEF PAT WITH A NEW CHILI POT... YOU ALL ENJOY THE CHAIR!

MERYL, THIS IS THE MOST COMFORTABLE CHAIR I'VE EVER SAT ON!

REALLY, MRS. SALTER? ME NEXT!

BBRING

DARN, THERE'S THE BELL.

≷GRUMBLE!≶

HOW AM I GOING TO TEACH THOSE CHUCKLE-HEADS WHEN ALL I CAN THINK ABOUT IS THIS CHAIR?

AH, CLASS IS *OVER*. ALRIGHT, JUST ME, MY TUNA, AND THIS CHAIR.

OH, HEY, DOODLE PIE! THIS CHAIR REALLY IS SWEETER THAN HONEY.

≋GROAN!≋ I'LL JUST COME BACK LATER.

TIME FOR SOME *BOLHOFNER* TIME.

SORRY, BOLHOFNER. YA SNOOZE, YA LOSE.

≋GRRR!≋ WHATEVER, *COACH KECK*.

AFTER THAT LAST EXHAUSTING CLASS, I *NEED* THAT CHAIR.

SERIOUSLY, MERYL. AGAIN?

WELL, ACTUALLY...

END

THE LOUD HOUSE
3 IN 1
#1

THE LOUD HOUSE
3 IN 1
#2

THE LOUD HOUSE
3 IN 1
#3

THE LOUD HOUSE
3 IN 1
#4

THE LOUD HOUSE
3 IN 1
#5

COMING SOON

THE CASAGRANDES
#1
"We're All Familia"

THE CASAGRANDES
#2
"Anything for Familia"

THE CASAGRANDES
#3
"Brand Stinkin' New"

THE CASAGRANDES
3 IN 1
#1

THE LOUD HOUSE
WINTER SPECIAL

THE LOUD HOUSE
SUMMER SPECIAL

THE LOUD HOUSE
LOVE OUT LOUD
SPECIAL

THE LOUD HOUSE
BACK TO SCHOOL
SPECIAL

WATCH OUT FOR PAPERCUTZ ™

Welcome to THE LOUD HOUSE BACK TO SCHOOL SPECIAL, brought to you by Papercutz, those scholarly souls dedicated to publishing great graphic novels for all ages. I'm Jim Salicrup, Editor-in-Chief and Teacher's Pet Peeve, here to suggest a few other Papercutz publications you may want to check out.

It seems that everyone has a different point of view regarding school. That, of course, makes sense, as everyone has their own unique experience of going to school. Every school is different. Every teacher is different. And every student is different. Just as every member of the Loud family is different. It's easy to imagine what each Loud would consider their favorite subject. For example, Luna would love Music and Lynn would excel in Gym. It should come as no surprise that my favorite subjects were English and Art. I've spent most of my life working in comics, which are basically words and pictures together. I was lucky to have had great teachers (such as Mrs. Crooks and Mr. Wolf) and suspect that in the future Lincoln is going to look back fondly on Mr. Bolhofner.

Lincoln and his friends may not realize what wonderful opportunities they have being back in school. While different schools offer different classes, it's great to get the chance to learn a foreign language. I sure wish I paid more attention when I took French class—now I edit graphic novels for Papercutz that were originally written in French, and I have to rely on our excellent translators to understand them.

One advantage in school that I share with Lincoln and Clyde is that because we all love comics, we have better than average reading skills. Imagine that! THE LOUD HOUSE graphic novels you get because you enjoy the show and characters, actually is helping you in school! Whether you're reading THE SMURFS or THE LOUD HOUSE, you're reading—and that puts you ahead of students who don't read anything other than what they're told to read in school.

Papercutz prouldly publishes several graphic novel series about schools or in which schools are prominently featured. DANCE CLASS is a long-running (or should I say long-dancing?) series about a dance school, focusing on three students, Lucie, Alia, and Julie. Written by Béka and drawn by Crip, the stories appeal to everyone, whether they're interested in dance or not. The wonderful thing about this school is that all the students choose to go there. They're all passionate about learning to dance and to express themselves creatively. That's how I felt in Art and English classes.

In SCHOOL FOR EXTRATERRESTRIAL GIRLS by Jeremy Whitley, writer, and Jamie Noguchi, artist, a young girl is taken away to a secret government school because she's an alien. While it's not uncommon to feel like you don't belong, imagine what it's like to find out you're from another planet.

Then there's a school for magical flying unicorns featured in the series MELOWY, by Cortney Powell, writer, and Ryan Jampole, artist. This is closer to the fantasy school that many dream of going to. Closer to reality is the school in GEEKY F@B 5, written by Lucy and Liz Lareau, and illustrated by Ryan Jampole. It's about five girls who set out to prove that anything is possible when girls, in this case, stick together.

The schools we see in THE LOUD HOUSE BACK TO SCHOOL SPECIAL are a bit over-the-top, poking gentle fun at all types of teachers and students. In real life, a good teacher can have an awesome impact on you, changing your life in a positive way. We hope this graphic novel made the grade with you, and that you'll come back for more fun with THE LOUD HOUSE in both the regular Papercutz graphic novel series and on Nickelodeon. But do me a personal favor? Make sure you get your homework done first, okay?

Class dismissed,

Jim

STAY IN TOUCH!

EMAIL: salicrup@papercutz.com
WEB: papercutz.com
TWITTER: @papercutzgn
INSTAGRAM: @papercutzgn
FACEBOOK: PAPERCUTZGRAPHICNOVELS
FANMAIL: Papercutz, 160 Broadway, Suite 700,
            East Wing, New York, NY 10038

Go to papercutz.com and sign up for the free Papercutz e-newsletter!